THE BIG BOOK OF FAVOURITE

IRISH

MYTHS

AND

LEGENDS

Gill Books
Hume Avenue, Park West, Dublin 12

www.gillbooks.ie

Gill Books is an imprint of M.H. Gill & Co.

Copyright © Teapot Press Ltd 2021

ISBN: 978-0-7171-9085-0

This book was created and produced by Teapot Press Ltd

Text by Joe Potter
Illustrated by Erin Brown
Edited by Fiona Biggs
Designed by Tony Potter

Printed in PRC

This book is typeset in Bembo Roman and Girlstory Script

THE BIG BOOK OF FAVOURITE

IRISH MYTHS AND LEGENDS

Stories retold by
Joe Potter

Illustrated by
Erin Brown

Gill Books

Contents

Introduction

This book includes some of the classic myths and legends of Irish folklore. The stories of love, magic, mystery and mayhem will enchant and entertain children of all ages, as they have done for generations. There are stories of clever and famous warriors, giants, jealous queens, mystical creatures and more. Irish story telling comes from a long and powerful oral tradition, so reading these tales out loud can be an enjoyable way to conjure up their magic in children's imaginations. Some of the names in the stories can be difficult to pronounce. A simple guide is printed below to help those unfamiliar with Irish words to read the stories either to themselves or out loud.

Pronunciation Guide

Aengus Óg	*Ayn-gus Oh-g*	Fedlimid Mac Daill	*Fey-li-meed Mock Dal*
Ailill	*A-leel*	Fergas Mac Róich	*Fur-gus Mock Row-uch*
Áinle	*Awn-le*	Fiacal	*Fee-a-call*
Aodh	*Ay*	Finnbhennach	*Fin-ven-ock*
Aoibh	*Eve*	Finnéigeas	*Finn-ay-gus*
Aoife	*Ee-fa*	Fionn Mac Cumhall	*Fee-yon Ma Cool*
Ardán	*Ar-dawn*	Fionnuala	*Fin-oo-la*
Benandonner	*Ben-an-don-er*	Glenbann	*Glenn-ban*
Bobdal	*Bob-dal*	Goll Mac Morna	*Gull Mock More-na*
Caomhóg	*Kway-vogue*	Gráinne	*Graw-nya*
Cathbad	*Cath-bud*	Labhraí Loingseach	*Lauw-ree Long-shuck*
Cúchulainn	*Coo-cull-un*	Leabharcham	*Lauw-er-come*
Diarmuid Ó Duibhne	*Deer-mid O Gwiv-na*	Lugh	*Loo*
Dónal	*Doe-null*	Maeve	*Mayve*
Fedelm	*Fidelm*	Naoise	*Nee-sha*
		Niamh	*Nee-uv*
		Oisín	*Ush-een*
		Samhain	*Sow-in*
		Tír na nÓg	*Teer Na Nogue*
		Tuatha Dé Danann	*Too-a-ha Day Da-nan*
		Uisneach	*Ish-nuck*

The Children of Lir

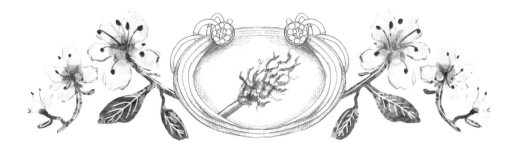

Long, long ago there lived a great king called Lir who had four children; a daughter named Fionnuala, a son called Aodh and twin brothers called Fiachra and Conn.

After the twins were born great tragedy fell upon Lir's house when his wife Aoibh died of a terrible sickness. Lir and his children were devastated and they mourned her for many moons. As time went on, however, Lir became lonely. More importantly, he felt his children needed a mother, so he decided to remarry. Unfortunately the king was a shallow man. The bride he found was beautiful of face but black of heart, and a black heart loves to a dark beat. Her name was Aoife. In her way she loved the king very much, but she did not love his children. Aoife had never wanted to be a mother and soon after the marriage she became jealous of her stepchildren.

"Lir shows those little brats far too much attention," Aoife spat into her mirror one night. "All his attention should be for me. I am his new bride, after all."

Over the next few days Aoife tried to draw Lir's attention away from them but he loved his children too dearly. He played all manner of games with them and he would listen to their singing for hours.

Jealousy rose and rose in Aoife until it was positively bubbling over. In a rage she decided that the children needed to be dealt with; she would get back the king's attention at any cost. She plotted and plotted, coming up with scheme after scheme until she found the perfect one.

She waited until the hottest day of the summer and called upon Lir, who was poring over papers in his study.

"My husband, you must be parched in this heat. Why not have a cold glass of wine?" she said, holding out a chilled glass.

Lir had been working for hours and his focus had been drifting for some time, "Why not?" said the king. "One small break can do no harm."

Aoife gave the king the glass of wine and he drank deeply. The start of her plan worked. As soon as he finished the glass his eyelids began to flutter. Aoife took the glass from his hand and she stroked his hair.

"There, my husband, sleep now." And the king fell into a deep, heavy sleep before her eyes.

As soon as she was sure Lir wouldn't wake, Aoife roused the four children, who were drowsing in the afternoon heat.

"Good afternoon my dear, dear little ones," she said, ever so quietly so as not to wake the king. "It's a beautiful day and the castle lake looks ever so inviting."

"Where's papa?" asked Fionnuala, who was shrewd and did not trust Aoife.

"Why, he's asleep of course. Your father is tired from his kingly duties, let's let him rest." The children loved the lake so they all agreed they should go down and bathe.

Down at the lake Aoife led the children into the water.

"Come now, children, cool yourselves," she said with a twisted grin. The children all waded out into the shallows. They began to splash water over each other, laughing uproariously.

As soon as their backs were turned Aoife took out a magical wand and cast a spell over the children.

In a flash of white light the children were transformed into four beautiful swans. They screamed at the sight of their beaks and feathers. "What has happened to us?" cried Fionnuala to her brothers.

Aoife spoke from upon the bank, "I am learned in the magical arts and I have cursed you. This will be your form for the next 900 years. Three hundred you shall spend here upon this lake. The next 300 years you will spend on the Sea of Moyle and the final 300 years you will pass on the Isle of Glora. The only thing that will break the spell is the sound of church bells."

"Why have you done this to us?" cried the children in unison.

"Because your father is mine and mine alone. Enjoy the next 900 years!" said Aoife, as she walked away laughing.

When the king woke he went around the house looking for his children. When he could not find them anywhere inside he walked into the grounds calling their names.

"Fionnuala? Aodh? Fiachra? Conn? Where are you?"

"We're here, Father!" Fionnuala called back. "We're in the lake."

He rounded the corner to the lake but could only see four swans paddling towards him.

"Father, Father! It's us!" Fionnuala said.

The king, dumbfounded, nearly fell backwards. "My children! What has happened to you?"

"Aoife has placed a terrible curse on us, Father," said the twins together.

The swans all bowed their long necks in misery.

Lir ran back to his castle as fast as his legs would carry him.

"Aoife! Aoife!" he yelled, crashing through the castle doors. Aoife was waiting at the top of the stairs. "Yes, my husband?" she said innocently.

"Aoife, what have you done to my children?" Lir demanded.

"Don't you see, Lir? I have done this for us. Now you can just be with me where you belong."

Lir sank to his knees in despair. "Please, put them right, I beg of you."

But Aoife was cold and was determined that if she could not have the king no one would. The king pleaded and pleaded but she refused. In the end the king lost his temper and banished Aoife from his kingdom for ever.

Lir searched high and low for someone to remove the curse from his children. He sought out wizards and warlocks, doctors and apothecaries, but none could break the spell. Aoife's magic was too powerful. Finally he was forced to accept that his children would remain as swans for the next 900 years.

Lir spent the rest of his life with his children by the lake, talking to them and listening to them sing, until he grew old and died. The swans were heartbroken. They could no longer sing and they could not even talk for their sorrow.

Three hundred long years passed and the time came for the children to fly to the Sea of Moyle. After a day there the swans thought longingly of their father's lake.

The sea was a harsh and stormy place, with little food to eat. The wild waves pulled the swans hither and thither and smashed their beautiful bodies against the sharp rocks. Time crawled by there and the years passed in misery.

When at long last 300 more years had passed the swans left for the Isle of Glora. They arrived at a saltwater lake and their time there was much happier. The water was calm, the air was warm and there was plenty of food. However, the swans were tired and old and they had grown very lonely. They had lingered in the mortal world too long and they ached to be with their father again. The next 300 years felt like a thousand. But pass they did, until one day the swans heard the far-off ringing of a bell.

"What's that sound?" asked the twins.

"It's a bell," said Fionnuala.

The children had lived for so long the curse was a distant memory. Aoife's prophecy came back to Fionnuala like a fragment of a half-forgotten dream.

"The bell! My brothers, this is the end of our plight," she shouted.

Ancient and frail, the swans swam towards the sound as fast as they could. At the bank they came across a little church. The sound of the bell died away inside and out walked an old monk called Caomhóg.

Caomhóg stood in amazement as the four swans swam up to him singing with human voices. The swans sung joyously, waiting to be transformed, but nothing happened. Fionnuala stopped singing and told Caomhóg of the curse upon them.

"Please sir, ring your bell again, for we wish to be human again."

Caomhóg hastened inside and rang the bell again but still nothing happened. The swans looked at each other in despair.

"I am most sorry," said Caomhóg. "Please come into my house and I will feed and bathe you."

The swans accepted gladly. That night they ate well and lay by a warm fire.

Unfortunately, Caomhóg was not the only one who knew of Lir's children.

The king of Connacht had heard about the singing swans. He knew he must have them for himself, for what other king in the land had singing swans?

The king travelled many miles to the Isle of Glora but when he reached the lake he saw only common birds. The only sight nearby was the church. While passing the windows, the king saw Caomhóg feeding the four swans by the fire. He pounded on the door.

"How may I help you?" asked Caomhóg when he opened the door.

"I demand you give me those swans. I am the king of Connacht and I need them for my castle."

Caomhóg refused flatly. He tried to shut the door in the king's face, but the king was strong and much younger than Caomhóg. He forced the door open and barged his way into the church. In his haste he knocked over a pail of holy water, dousing the swans with the liquid. The king kicked the pail aside and went to grab the swans. Just as he touched them Aoife's spell broke. The king backed away as the swans' feathers all fell out.

Before his very eyes the swans vanished completely, leaving four extremely old, wrinkled people on the hearth. The king fled in horror.

Fionnuala put her arms around her brothers, delighted to be human once more.

"Caomhóg, we are 900 years old now and we shall soon die. Before we go please would you baptise us so we can be with our father once more?"

Caomhóg did as she asked and baptised the four ancient people. Soon afterwards they died of old age and he buried them in one grave. The children were now at rest. That night Caomhóg dreamt that he saw four swans flying up through the clouds. He knew that the children of Lir were now safe with their mother and father.

Fionn Mac Cumhaill and the Salmon of Knowledge

O nce upon a half-forgotten time there lived a boy. A boy who would one day grow up to be a great leader of the Fianna. A warrior. Fionn Mac Cumhaill. His father was Cumhall, leader of the Fianna, the king's special army. Cumhall was the mightiest of them all, but the other warriors were jealous and plotted against him. One day, they seized their chance and murdered him.

Cumhall's wife was so afraid for her baby son that she took Fionn to a cave in the Sliabh Bloom Mountains to two women called Bobdal and Fiacal: one was a druid and the other a warrior. They took care of Fionn, taught him spells and how to defend himself.

But before a boy can use a sword he must use his mind, for the mind is mightier than a thousand swords. If he was to be a great leader one day he must have a great mind, so the women sent him to live with the wisest of all men. Some called him Finn Eces, others Finnéigeas, but there was no mistaking him. Everyone knew him. He was the poet who lived on the banks of the River Boyne, a sage, the man who knew things. He knew the secrets of the birds and the planets and the stars and more, much, much more. And when he spoke his words were beautiful, dancing and jumping around each other, picked out of paradise to fall on your ear.

And so it was that Bobdal and Fiacal sent Fionn alone across ancient Ireland to seek out the famous Finnéigeas.

Fionn was only a boy but he travelled for many miles to find the old man. After three days and three nights of walking across the country he reached the River Boyne. Fionn had never seen Finnéigeas before but he knew him when he saw him. The old man was sitting under an old chestnut tree on the bank, fishing in the river. He was far away but Fionn could hear him reciting poetry to the water. His appearance gave him away. With his white robe and sandals, long white beard and bushy eyebrows he looked like the wisest man in the world. Fionn ran over to Finnéigeas but was suddenly struck with nerves, unable to talk. Finnéigeas looked up and considered Fionn kindly.

"So far you have come over hill and dale, over river and ford and meadow pale. So far you have come across valley and peak, tell me, boy, what do you seek?"

"Wisdom, O wise Finnéigeas."

"Wisdom is a hard fish to catch. She wriggles in your hands and slaps you in the face, gets you all wet and jumps all over the place."

Fionn thought Finnéigeas might be a bit mad, but he was clever enough to know that a spark of madness can often hide wisdom.

"But wisdom is not everyone's game," said Finnéigeas. "Tell me, boy, what is your name?"

"Fionn Mac Cumhaill."

Finnéigeas thought for a moment. He knew the family that Fionn came from. He knew the boy would one day be a great leader and it would be wise to create a wise leader. However, Finnéigeas had a problem. He spent so much time thinking on the bank and reciting poetry that his house was falling into ruin. There were dirty pots and

pans everywhere, and old books and scrolls littered the floor. There was half-eaten food, spiderwebs and more. There were dead flowers in a vase, smelly things on the table and mud on the door! All manner of mess infested his house. Unfortunately, Finnéigeas hated cooking and cleaning and all things involving ordinary work, and besides, he couldn't think well while tidying. So Finnéigeas thought for a while, then announced a plan for Fionn.

"I will tell you what I know in exchange for your time. Will you cook and clean and keep my house in line?"

"Most certainly, wise Finnéigeas, I will," said Fionn, jumping for joy.

And so it began. Fionn cleaned Finnéigeas's house every day from top to bottom. He cooked Finnéigeas meals for breakfast, lunch and dinner. He washed his clothes, he did his ironing, he scrubbed and swept and a million things besides. Finnéigeas marvelled at the boy. However quickly he could make a mess, Fionn could clean it up faster.

Fionn worked so hard because he had endless questions in his heart. As soon as he had finished a task he would run out to Finnéigeas on the bank and ask a question about the world. Finnéigeas answered his questions as thoroughly as Fionn cleaned the house. He told him the secrets of the birds and the planets and the stars. He told him stories from every corner of the world. He told him fables and fairy tales and every poem he knew until Fionn could recite them back word perfect. But the more Finnéigeas told him the more Fionn wanted to know.

Finnéigeas was a very wise man indeed and he knew a great many things, but he did not know everything. There came a time when Finnéigeas simply couldn't answer any more of Fionn's questions.

"Is there a way to know everything?" Fionn asked, when Finnéigeas could no longer answer him.

Finnéigeas had once asked this question himself and it was the very reason he now lived on the banks of the Boyne. The story was as old to Finnéigeas as Finnéigeas is to you. It was said that the chestnut trees overhanging the river were once magical. One autumn, when the chestnuts fell into the river they were gobbled up by a salmon. The salmon instantly gained all the knowledge in the world. And so, according to prophecy, the one who would catch and eat the Salmon of Knowledge would gain the knowledge for themselves.

Finnéigeas had moved to the bank in hope of catching the Salmon of Knowledge. He had fished the river every day for years and years. He caught pike and trout, bass and perch, eel and carp and shad and snapper, but not a nibble from the Salmon of Knowledge. Decades passed and Finnéigeas began to wonder if there even was a Salmon of Knowledge.

"There is a way, it lies in the pool, the Salmon of Knowledge, I've heard it called. If you wish to know all, catch it and eat it and your mind will be filled."

Finnéigeas passed his fishing rod over to Fionn. The boy settled by the river and waited and waited for the Salmon of Knowledge. But he had no more luck than Finnéigeas. He caught pike and trout, bass

and perch, eel and carp and shad and snapper, but not a nibble from the Salmon of Knowledge. Fionn was not patient like Finnéigeas and, after only a couple of days he threw down the fishing rod in a rage.

"This is impossible, Finnéigeas, the salmon does not exist!"

Finnéigeas sighed and picked up the fallen fishing rod as Fionn stormed back into the house. He spoke to the river.

"One more time I'll cast my line, if he doesn't bite, the knowledge will never be mine."

Finnéigeas picked out his brightest lure and hooked a particularly juicy worm. He cast out with a firm hand far into the river and waited, and waited. He waited so long that he fell asleep. He slept for a long time. Hours later he was suddenly wrenched out of his dreams. Something was pulling on the fishing line. Finnéigeas scrambled to reel in the fish. He reeled and reeled with all his might. He twisted this way and that till his muscles were sore, and then, with one huge effort, he yanked the fish from the depths of the water. Finnéigeas fell backwards as the huge salmon landed in his lap.

"I've got it, I've caught it, that fabled fish! Fionn, come quick and put it in a dish!"

Fionn ran out of the house and lit a fire as fast as he could. He was a little upset he hadn't caught the salmon himself, but Finnéigeas promised him he'd tell him all he knew once he'd eaten the fish. However, he had some words of caution for him, for the knowledge could only pass to one.

"I caught it boy, the knowledge is mine. Do not take one bite, one morsel. Heed my rhyme."

While Finnéigeas ran off to fetch more firewood Fionn cooked

the fish for Finnéigeas and didn't eat a single bite. When Finnéigeas returned Fionn had laid out the cooked salmon for him.

Finnéigeas sat down and grabbed his knife and fork and was just about to dig in when he noticed something in Fionn's eyes. There was a wisdom in their depths that he had not seen before.

"Tell me, boy, did you take a bite? There's something in your eyes, I see a new light."

"I did not!" protested Fionn.

"You have not even tasted its skin? I see knowledge deep within."

"I have not!" replied Fionn, "but while turning the salmon on the spit I burnt my thumb and put it in my mouth to ease the pain."

Finnéigeas's heart sank. "You have tasted the Salmon of Knowledge all the same, and upon you all the world's wisdom shall rain."

He then ordered Fionn to eat all of the fish. However, when he had eaten every last bite the boy didn't feel any wiser than he had before. The only new knowledge he had was from Finnéigeas himself.

"I don't feel any different, wise Finnéigeas."

Finnéigeas was lost in sadness. He had been so close to acquiring all the knowledge in the world, his heart's greatest desire. However, he roused himself and plumbed the depths of his mind.

"You put your thumb to your mouth to ease the pain, place it there once more and the knowledge you will gain."

Fionn did as Finnéigeas said. He put his thumb in his mouth and suddenly all the knowledge of the world rushed into his mind. He knew now and then, north and south. He knew here and there, east and west. He saw beyond the planets, beyond the stars, beyond everything that Finnéigeas knew.

"It worked, Finnéigeas! I know all! I have seen beyond, farther than I could imagine." Fionn was overjoyed. All he had to do now to know all the secrets of the world was suck his thumb. However, now that he knew everything Fionn felt lost.

"What should I do now, Finnéigeas?" he asked.

"You must go. There is nothing more I can teach you. Fulfil your destiny boy, I beseech you."

And so it was that Fionn left Finnéigeas and grew up to be a poet, a warrior and the wisest and greatest of all Fianna leaders. Finnéigeas went back to his poetry and sharing all the knowledge he possessed. There was no shame in being the second wisest man in the world.

The King with the Donkey Ears

Many many years ago there lived a king named Labhraí Loingseach. Labhraí Loingseach was powerful and was feared throughout the land. He had miles upon miles of land, he had castles and mansions, whole towns and villages. He had gold and riches that one could only dream of, but he also had a secret, a most embarrassing secret that he would rather die than have people discover. The king had huge ears – in fact, they were exactly like those of a donkey. They were long and grey and hairy and they protruded right over the top of his head.

To hide them the king always had a very special haircut, styled just so that the ears could not be seen. Once a year he sent out for a barber. After the barber had cut his hair the king had him immediately put to death so he could never reveal his terrible secret. As the years went on, though, people began to notice the disappearances of all the barbers. In the end there were very few barbers left in Ireland. If the king's messenger arrived at your house and demanded you cut his hair, why, you'd never be seen again! As a consequence everyone's hair grew very long and shaggy.

However, some people are destined to become this or that despite the danger. In Loingseach's kingdom there lived a young man named Dónal, whose passion was cutting hair. Dónal's mother lived in constant fear for her only son. She issued dire warning after dire warning but Dónal was not deterred. Nothing was going to stop him from being a barber.

"The king could send for you right this moment, Dónal, and then you'd be gone for ever!" said Dónal's mother one night.

"Nonsense, mother," he said, laughing, "it's just an old wife's tale. Why on earth would the king kill his barbers? If he is it's because they're not doing a good enough job and I am the best barber in the land."

"Oh, my poor son, I'd even prefer you to be a knight. It would be safer than being a barber!"

Just then there was a knock at the door. Dónal's mother looked through the window and clutched her heart.

"It's the king's messenger, hide!" Dónal ignored her and opened the door with a cheery smile to let the man in.

"I come on behalf of King Labhraí Loingseach," said the man importantly. "Madam, I have come to bring your son before the king. He has a very special job for him to perform. I'm sure you realise what an honour this is. We leave immediately."

Dónal's mother wailed and tried to grab hold of her son.

"Please don't go, Dónal, please!"

"I have to mother, it's the king's orders."

Although it broke Dónal's heart to do it he had to leave his mother weeping on the floor as the messenger took him away. But Dónal's mother was not about to give up yet. As soon as they were gone she stopped crying and jumped on her horse. She rode straight to the castle as fast as she could and pleaded her case before the king.

"Please, my king, my son is all I have in this world. I am getting old and if you kill him there will be no one to care for me. He is a good boy and a wonderful son. I beg you, spare him."

The king was not a nice man; in fact, he was downright evil, but Dónal's mother reminded him of his own mother and he felt rather sorry for her. He thought long and hard before he answered.

"I will spare your son's life on one condition. He must promise to never utter a word of anything he sees in this castle, not to any living person. If he can make this pledge and stay true to it his life will be spared."

The next day Dónal was called into the king's chambers. The king ordered all of his men out until it was just him and Dónal.

"I have spoken to your mother," said the king.

"Yes, my king, I promise I will not utter a word of anything I see in this castle, not to any living person."

"Promise?" asked the king. Dónal nodded in fright. "All right, then," said the king, taking off his crown and shaking out his hair. The huge donkey ears were revealed and Dónal gasped. The king eyed Dónal angrily and Dónal quickly set about cutting his hair.

Whatever Dónal thought he might see, it wasn't a pair of donkey ears. He was careful not to cut the ears but he did the job as quickly as possible then raced out of the king's chambers. He ran all the way home with his mouth clamped tight and ignored anyone who tried to talk to him. Dónal's mother was delighted to see him.

"Dónal!" she cried, hugging her son. "You're alive, you're alive! So it went all right with the king then?"

Dónal didn't dare open his mouth but just nodded and went straight to bed. For three days he spoke to no one and stayed shut up in his room. Dónal's mother knew something was wrong with her son but she didn't dare question him further. Although she was very relieved to have her son back he was never quite the same again. He slept little and ate less. He also hardly spoke and seldom wanted to cut people's hair anymore. After months and months of this Dónal's mother decided to take him to a druid to see if he could help. But the druid took one look at Dónal and sighed.

"I cannot help him. He is holding on to a secret deep inside and he will not improve until he lets it go."

"What do you mean, O wise druid?" Dónal's mother asked.

"He must tell someone the secret," replied the druid, "otherwise it will eat him up from the inside."

"Alas, he cannot reveal the secret he carries to anyone. The secret belongs to the king and he has vowed never to speak a word of it, not to any living person."

The wise druid meditated for a while.

"I have a solution to the boy's problem! He must go into the forest and find a tree to tell. He can whisper the secret to the leaves. That way no other soul will hear and he will not have broken his promise, for a tree is no living person."

Dónal followed the druid's advice and went to the forest at once. When he arrived he walked deep into the trees, to make sure no one could overhear him. Right at the heart of the forest he found a beautiful willow tree by a stream. He sat on the bank and the willow's leaves swayed in front of his face. Dónal leaned in very close and began to whisper his secret.

With every word it felt as though poison was being siphoned out of him. The weight lifted and lifted until it was gone and Dónal felt quite himself again.

That afternoon the willow tree had another visitor. A musician from the king's castle had broken his harp and was in need of a replacement.

He searched the land but could not find a harp with the perfect sound. In the end he decided the only solution was

to make his own so he went into the forest to find some wood. As he was the finest player in the land he decided only the finest wood would do for his harp. He searched for hours in the forest and when he came across the willow he saw that it was perfect. He chopped off a branch and fashioned his new harp that very night.

The harpist was delighted when he'd finished. The harp was his most beautiful creation. He ran off to the great hall to play for the king immediately. There were a great many people in the hall that evening. There were chieftains and ladies, princes and druids and a great many common folk besides.

"Music!" The king cried when the harpist entered. "Excellent!" The harpist set to playing at once. He struck his fingers against the strings.

Now, wise as Dónal's druid was, he had not considered that while a tree is no living person it is still a living thing. The secret blossomed through the wood and, as the musician played, the harp emitted its own song. Strange music filled the hall.

"The king, the king has donkey ears.

The king, the king has terrible fears.

The king, the king you all should know,

On top of his head they do grow.

Long and grey and furry too,

This is the secret he keeps from you."

Loingseach jumped up from his throne and ran at the harpist in a furious rage. He tried to wrestle the harp out of the musician's hands and, in the commotion, his crown went flying off his head. The king fell backwards and his donkey ears were revealed.

Silence filled the hall. Everyone could see the ears quite plainly. The king looked around at everyone's shocked faces and suddenly he began to laugh. The people laughed too and the harpist helped him up.

"Don't worry, my lord, no ones cares about your donkey ears."

As the evening wore on the king saw that the harpist was right. Nobody seemed to take much notice of his ears. The secret was

33

out and there was no point trying to keep it anymore. The king felt happier and calmer than he ever had before. After that day the kingdom too was a happier place, especially for the barbers. Thanks to Dónal they would never be in danger again.

The Cattle Raid of Cooley

Long ago King Conor Mac Nessa ruled over Ulster and Queen Maeve and her husband Ailill ruled over Connacht.

One day Maeve came back to the castle with a brand new set of armour and proclaimed it to be finer than anything her husband owned. Ailill was outraged and quickly fetched a portrait of himself he had had painted.

"Your armour is very beautiful indeed, my wife, but it cannot compare to my painting. It took the artist six months to complete."

Maeve hastened to her closet and plucked out a gown made from the finest silk in the land.

"This is finer than any painting," she said. "It took four women a year to make."

On and on this went, with Maeve and Ailill comparing clothes and jewellery, chariots and coaches, even their horses in the stables.

"My mare is far more beautiful than yours, Ailill," she taunted.

Ailill thought for a moment and then took his wife to the field behind their castle.

"I bet you don't have anything as fine as him!" Ailill pointed to his prize bull.

The bull was enormous and muscly with a shiny white coat unrivalled by any Maeve had seen. She did not want to admit it but her husband was perfectly right. The bull was finer than anything she owned. Maeve stormed off in a jealous rage.

This would not stand. There was no way Maeve was going to concede defeat. She screamed throughout the castle for her messenger.

"Mac Roth! Mac Roth!"

Fergus Mac Roth came running to her at once.

"Mac Roth, do you know of any bull in Ireland that could rival my husband's?"

"Why yes, my lady," he said, "I know of a bull not only better but twice as good as your husband's. In Ulster, Daire of Cooley owns a fearsome beast. They call it the Brown Bull of Cooley."

Maeve sent Fergus Mac Roth with a company of men to Ulster immediately. She offered 50 cows and a large piece of Connacht land for the prize bull. Daire agreed to the offer at once. Indeed, he was so delighted with the deal that he held an enormous feast for Fergus and his men. The feast was a joyous occasion with much dancing and singing and Daire was having a wonderful time until he overheard a drunken Connacht soldier nearby.

"Daire would have been a fool to refuse Maeve, even if she'd only offered a milk cow! She would have just taken the bull by force if he'd said no."

Daire was furious. He stood on his chair and yelled across the hall, "The deal's off! If Maeve wants my bull she'll have to come take it by force!"

So the men arrived back at Connacht empty-handed. When Fergus told Maeve the deal was off she was incensed.

"Mac Roth, gather up all the men in the castle. We're marching to Ulster to get that bull!" she said, stamping her feet in rage.

As Fergus gathered the army Maeve's personal fortune teller Fedelm came running into her chambers.

"My Queen! Before you send your army for Ulster I must tell you of a most disturbing vision I have just seen."

Maeve rounded on her. "Make it quick, Fedelm. We leave for Ulster as soon as the horses are ready."

Fedelm raised her voice dramatically and said;

"I see him in the shadows,

Taking bite after bite,

But try as you may, try as you might,

You will never be able to fight.

Not him, not he, the mighty one

Cúchulainn, Sualdam's son!

Whole hosts will he destroy,

no matter what magic you deploy.

Heed my words, hear my song,

Hold back your men or their lives will not last long."

But Maeve did not care. She was far too angry to heed Fedelm's words. And so she marched off with her army for Ulster without a backward glance. Fury led her on and on. She would have her prize if it cost her the whole of Connacht. King Conor Mac Nessa heard the army was on the move and sent out his Red Branch Knights to meet them.

While on the road Maeve ordered one of her magicians to put a spell on the Ulster army. As they were marching the Red Branch Knights fell to sickness one by one, all apart from their greatest warrior, Cúchulainn. As Maeve's army marched towards Ulster Cúchulainn terrorised them. Hiding in the trees along their route he used a slingshot to kill hundreds of Maeve's men.

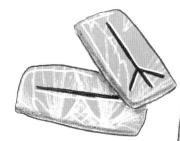

38

Whenever he saw a straggler on the flank Cúchulainn would rush forward and strike the man down. Little by little Maeve's army was whittled down. Fearing Cúchulainn would kill her whole army she sent a messenger to him, offering him land and money to join her army. Cúchulainn declined all offers and said he would stop only if he could fight Maeve's warriors one by one. Maeve agreed. This Cúchulainn had proven himself fierce, but surely one of her warriors could defeat him. Cúchulainn met Maeve's army by the River Dee.

When the men saw Cúchulainn standing alone they laughed. He was still a young man of only 17 and he did not look particularly fierce in the cold light of day. Maeve sent her warriors to attack Cúchulainn one by one but he defeated them all until a hundred men lay dead at his feet.

Maeve ordered the next man to fight Cúchulainn but he hung back in fear. In desperation Maeve called for her greatest warrior.

"Ferdia! Attack him now!"

Ferdia stepped forward, but told Maeve he could not attack Cúchulainn.

"We grew up together, my lady. He is my brother and a great friend."

Maeve was well aware of this so she offered Ferdia riches beyond his wildest dreams.

She even offered him her daughter's hand in marriage, but Ferdia was not swayed. It was then that Maeve came up with a wicked lie.

"Ferdia, Cúchulainn has been saying you are a coward. He says you are hiding behind my skirts like a little boy." This maddened Ferdia and he charged off to meet Cúchulainn.

For three days the two warriors fought in single combat. However, they were both so skilled at fighting that neither gained any advantage over the other. The men were still great friends. Each evening they sent parcels to each other containing food, drink and medicine to make sure the other was at his full strength.

At sunrise on the fourth day the two men met in the shallows of the River Dee. Metal clashed and the water splashed. They fought tirelessly but neither man could wound the other. The Ulster knights had by now recovered from their sickness. As they came running towards the river they saw Cúchulainn fighting. The men cheered loudly for their champion. Distracted, Cúchulainn looked around at the men cheering. Ferdia saw his chance and struck Cúchulainn across the chest. Cúchulainn fell to his knees and his sword went flying out of his hand. Seeing this, one of the Red Branch Knights threw a spear into the river. The spear floated towards Cúchulainn. Just as Ferdia was about to drive his sword into his friend, Cúchulainn grabbed the spear and put it through Ferdia's heart. Ferdia fell forward and Cúchulainn caught him. He felt no joy at winning, only sorrow as his friend died in his arms. The Red Branch Knights cheered and charged at Maeve's army. Disheartened by their champion's defeat the army retreated, running for the hills.

In all the commotion Maeve sneaked off to Daire's land with a few men and stole the Brown Bull of Cooley. Maeve saw that Fergus

Mac Roth had told no lie. The bull truly was twice as fine as her husband's. It was almost twice the size with a glistening coat and muscles that bulged from his legs and chest. Maeve was delighted. She had lost many men but the prize was well worth the sacrifice. She arrived back in Connacht in triumph.

"Make sure my bull is safe!" she commanded her men. "Put him in the pen and make sure no one sees him. If any Ulster men come to take him back, protect him with your lives!"

The brown bull was distressed and angry at being moved so far. As he was put in the pen he started bellowing. The deep booming noise woke Ailill's white bull Finnbhennach and he came charging out to defend his territory in a burning rage.

Fergus Mac Roth ran into the queen's chambers to tell her that the bulls were about to fight. Maeve came racing downstairs. This was even better than merely having the bull. Now, once and for all, they would see whose bull was the stronger, hers or Ailill's. All the warriors in the castle ran to the pen's fence to watch the mighty fight.

The duel lasted all night, with the bulls clashing over and over again, locking horns and stamping their feet. The brown bull was much larger but Finnbhennach was faster. For a time he managed to dodge the brown bull's blows by jumping this way and that, but in the end the brown bull overpowered him. With one mighty swipe of his horns the brown bull finally impaled Finnbhennach and the white bull died instantly.

Maeve and the men all cheered. Ailill looked on in horror at the demise of his prize bull.

"Well, my husband," Maeve said to Ailill, "I think we know now who has the finest possessions in the land."

The brown bull was still stomping and charging around the pen. Just then he started bellowing again. He turned in rage and charged straight through the fence and galloped home to Cooley. But his capture and the fight had left him weak and he had barely gone half a mile before he collapsed and his heart stopped.

Maeve, open-mouthed, watched the bull run off and die.

Ailill smiled and turned to his wife. "I think in the end dear, no one was a winner here."

Fionn and the Dragon

Long ago when Fionn Mac Cumhaill was approaching manhood, the time came for him to leave his mentor Finnéigeas. He had tasted the Salmon of Knowledge and there was no more Finnéigeas could teach him.

For many weeks Fionn wandered around Ireland seeking adventures. He searched high and low from Malin Head to Kinsale but found nothing. His life on the road was quiet and solitary and Fionn began to wonder if there were any more adventures to be had. One day he saw a band of chieftains and soldiers and ran over to greet them.

"Good day, men, tell me, what is your quest?" Fionn called to them.

"No quest," one of the chieftains said. "We are travelling to Tara for the great festival of Samhain. The great assembly is near."

Fionn's heart sank. He wanted to go into battle or fight a monster. The great assembly meant peace for six whole weeks. No man was even allowed to raise a weapon in Tara during that time. However, Fionn was weary and he greatly enjoyed feasting and singing.

"I shall join you, if I may?" said Fionn.

"Of course, if you want to risk it," said the chieftain, walking off.

Fionn joined the men and asked what the chieftain had meant by his comment.

One of the men spoke up. "Tara is a cursed place. Every year at the great assembly an evil daemon attacks the city."

"What sort of daemon?" asked Fionn.

"It comes in the form of a fire-breathing dragon, and sets all Tara aflame."

Another soldier piped up in a terrified voice, "They call him 'the Burner'. He is one of the Tuatha Dé Danann, one of the old gods themselves. He is a daemon of the underworld, straight from Mag Meall. We're all doomed!"

"But why have the Fianna not killed it?" asked Fionn. "They are the bravest soldiers in the land."

The soldier was tired of explaining. "Because the daemon flies over and plays sweet music that sends every soul to sleep. The magicians have tried to stop it but they are powerless," he said wearily.

"I could kill it," said Fionn loudly.

The soldier laughed, "Oh yes? And how are you going to fight it when you're asleep? No ordinary man could kill the daemon."

Fionn made no answer but he smiled, for he was no ordinary man.

By the time they reached Tara, Samhain had already started. The sun was going down behind the walls and Tara twinkled with lights.

As Fionn entered the castle he saw people dancing around fires and making offerings to the spirits and fairies. People laid food and gifts outside their houses in the hope that this year the daemon would leave Tara unscathed. People nearby started to sing.

Samhain, Samhain, let the spirits rain,

Oh, mercy we ask from you, Aillen,

Come to take our gifts and offers made,

Please accept the price as paid.

Come take our gold and most precious spoils

But leave our castle free from toils.

Fionn was alarmed. All around people looked frightened, almost cowering, and even the horses pawed the ground nervously. This would not stand. Samhain was a time of joy and peace, when people welcomed the spirits and fairies into the world with open arms.

Fionn ran off to find the great hall where the greatest warriors of Ireland were all seated with the king. Brave and fearless, Fionn bounded into the hall and approached the king's high table.

He eyed the Fianna's table and their leader Goll Mac Morna as he passed. Goll looked back with a strange light of recognition in his eye. Fionn looked away and cleared his throat before the king.

"Who approaches the high table so boldly?" asked the king, staring down at Fionn with a bored expression.

Fionn spoke up so all could hear. "I am Fionn, son of Cumhal."

The hall went quiet at his words and every eye turned towards Goll Mac Morna. Some years earlier he had killed Fionn's father. Goll shifted uncomfortably in his seat.

Fionn spoke again. "I have heard that an evil daemon plagues your castle."

"Yes, every year at the assembly for nine years, Aillen of the Flaming Breath has set fire to Tara. What of it?" said the king.

"I will slay the daemon for you," shouted Fionn. Several people laughed and even the king looked slightly amused. Although Fionn was tall and very strong he was still young and he had not yet grown a beard. "But I will only do it for a price."

"If you kill Aillen of the Flaming Breath you may have whatever you wish," said the king sarcastically.

Fionn looked Goll Mac Morna right in the eye. "I wish to be the leader of the Fianna."

"Done," said the king. "Kill this daemon for me and your wish is my command."

Fionn left the hall immediately to patrol the ramparts. As he climbed higher and higher he noticed people everywhere with drooping eyes. He could hear the distant magical music of the fairy world. The daemon must be near, he thought. The music was very beautiful. It was soothing and melodic and conjured up images of green fields and rolling waves in Fionn's mind. He suddenly felt tired and his knees slackened. He shook himself hard to clear his mind. He hurried on, determined to get to the daemon before the music took him.

Just then, somebody grabbed his arm and Fionn looked back. A soldier stood there holding a strange spear. The metal on it was engraved with runes and encrusted with dark stones and some silent power seemed to emanate from the weapon.

"I am Fiacha," said the man. "Your father was a dear friend of mine. For his sake I give you this spear of enchantment. It is said that the spear will protect against any spell, but no one in the castle knows its secret. I am sorry not to be of more help. But if you can work the spear no evil spell will be able to harm you."

Fionn tried to thank him but Fiacha had already walked away. As Fionn watched, Fiacha collapsed and fell into a deep sleep. The daemon Aillen was here. Fionn placed his magical thumb in his mouth and instantly he knew the spear's secret. He pressed the spear to his forehead and any drowsiness he felt left him. He could hear the sweet, poisonous music from Aillen's mouth but it had no effect on him. Up on the ramparts Fionn looked down and saw people all over the castle slumped in odd positions where they had fallen asleep. He alone stood tall. The sky was dark and still. Fionn's keen eyes scanned the horizon for Aillen. The music grew louder and louder, filling the whole castle. Then Fionn saw him, a monstrous dragon flying out of the clouds straight at him.

Aillen was a fearsome winged beast, twenty metres long with blood-red scales as hard as steel and long vicious teeth that glistened in the darkness. As he sped towards Fionn and the castle the daemon opened his jaws wide and spat a blistering jet of fire at Fionn. Fionn ducked and the flames missed him but set fire to a barrel. He noticed that Fiacha lay nearby and hurried over to put out the fire with his cloak.

Aillen spouted fire here and there. He set stables alight and incinerated market stalls. He melted iron statues and sent wagons flying. But Fionn was right behind him putting out every fire he saw.

He covered the flames with his cloak or doused them with water as fast as Aillen could set them alight. Aillen looked back in fury. Who was this mere human who seemed impervious to his music? He sang as loud as he could but the music had no effect. Incensed, Aillen flew straight at Fionn. Fionn stood his ground, taking careful aim. He knew the daemon's scales were too strong to pierce so he waited until Aillen was right upon him. The daemon's jaws opened, ready to eat Fionn whole. With all his might Fionn threw the magical spear.

His aim was true. He managed to pierce Aillen right under one of his blood-red scales. The daemon fell to the ground howling and lay writhing upon the ground. Without a second thought Fionn ran over and chopped off Aillen's head with his sword. A last jet of flame shot from Aillen's neck and then the daemon lay dead upon the ground. Fionn staggered back to the castle with the head and held it up in triumph. Very slowly people started to wake up. They wandered around in a daze, wondering why there was not more damage to the castle. The king ran out into the courtyard and saw Fionn with the dragon's head in his hand.

"You did it! My dear boy, I can never thank you enough," he said, wringing his hands.

All around people were cheering, shouting Fionn's name.

"What about our bargain?" asked Fionn.

"I am a man of my word," said the king. "You shall be the new leader of the Fianna as your father was before you. Goll Mac Morna," he called. "Step forward."

Goll appeared out of the crowd and stepped towards his king.

"Yes, your majesty?" he said.

"Goll, do you accept Fionn Mac Cumhaill as your new leader?"

Goll looked at Fionn then bowed his head. "I accept you as the leader of the Fianna. You have done what no other man could do. You are truly a hero." And Goll knelt down before Fionn.

One by one the other members of the Fianna emerged from the crowd and joined Goll on their knees before their new leader.

And so it was that Fionn Mac Cumhaill became the leader of the Fianna and led them to greater deeds than had ever been performed before. Fionn's Fianna will always be remembered in Ireland.

The Giant's Causeway

Many years ago there lived in a castle in Antrim the most famous warrior of all, named Fionn Mac Cumhaill, with his wife Una. He was the wisest and bravest man in Ireland. It was said he had the strength of 500 men and his voice could be heard for miles around. Over the sea in Scotland a giant named Benandonner had heard the stories of Fionn's valour. If stories were travelling right over the sea he must be very great indeed, thought Benandonner. This would not do. He knew he must defeat Fionn in combat so there was no doubt in anyone's mind who was the greater, in Scotland, in Ireland, in the whole world. No one would be thought greater than he.

Benandonner was a tremendous giant. He was as tall as an oak tree and his arms were as big as tree trunks. His hands could crush stone and his footfalls could cause avalanches. He was as broad as a house and as vicious as the ocean. All Scotland feared him. He was spoken about in whispers and the mere mention of his name shot terror into the hearts of even the bravest soul.

This was the way Benandonner liked things and this was the way they would stay. In a huge rage he stormed across Scotland to the Isle of Staffa.

Standing on the cliffs Benandonner could see the Irish coast in the distance. He filled his lungs with a great rumble that set the seagulls flying.

"Fionn Mac Cumhaill!" he yelled, louder than a thousand men, "I am Benandonner and I seek a fight with you, Fionn! If you refuse all Scotland and Ireland will know you are a coward and that I am the most fearsome being in these lands!"

From his castle in Antrim Fionn heard the voice upon the air. At first he thought it was the wind until he was quite sure that he heard his own name. Fionn ran to the seashore the better to hear the giant's voice. As he approached the rocks he heard the voice distinctly.

"I am Benandonner and I will crush you into the dirt, Fionn Mac Cumhaill! Fight me or be ever thought a coward!"

So a giant named Benandonner was challenging him to a fight, was he? Fionn had never backed away from a challenge in his life and he was not about to start now. He had fought armies and fire-breathing monsters; he was not afraid. Fionn filled his lungs and yelled back across the sea with all his might.

"Benandonner, I accept your challenge gladly! Don't go anywhere. I'll come straight over to you now!" And with that Fionn started heaving rocks up from the shore and casting them into the sea.

Once he could stand on one he started making a pathway. A most strange pathway it was too. All the rocks were black, some had six sides, some had eight and others more than ten.

The sea crashed around him trying to knock him this way and that, but Fionn fought through. One after another Fionn ripped up rocks and placed them in the sea, making his path longer and longer. Every stone created a step in the water, bringing Fionn ever closer to Scotland and to Benandonner. But the way was far and the task took many hours. Benandonner, who was getting tired by now, decided to lie down and get some rest. Working furiously, Fionn placed rock after rock, but by the time he reached the coast of Staffa Benandonner had fallen fast asleep. This was most fortunate for Fionn.

He had never seen Benandonner before and now that he did he could see that he was a monster. Fionn was exceptionally large himself but he was nothing compared to this giant. Even lying down Benandonner's chest rose higher than Fionn's head. Fionn scarpered. He ran back over his rocks and sprinted home to Ireland as fast as he could.

Fionn arrived at his castle breathless, with a wild look in his eye.

"Are you all right, darling?" Una asked.

"Um, yes, dear, but I may have done something foolish." Fionn proceeded to explain about Benandonner and the challenge he had unwittingly accepted.

"Oh dear," said Una. "How big did you say this giant was?"

"Una, he is fully ten times my own size, he is the biggest creature I have ever seen. His teeth are like bricks, his shoes are like sleds. He is so massive the ground shook as he snored."

"All right, all right," said Una. "You cannot beat him with your strength so you must beat him with your mind."

Fionn thought long and hard. How could he possibly outwit Benandonner? He walked round and round the castle hatching plans that flared and died in his mind immediately. Whatever he came up with seemed weak and feeble. Una too thought for hours but she could not think of any solution.

"Begosh, tricking an angry giant is no easy thing, Fionn," Una said hours later.

"But we must, my darling! Truly there is no way I can beat him. If he was standing he'd be taller than our castle! And time is running out. As soon as he's awake he'll run over my causeway straight here!" Fortunately, strong as her husband was, Una was as smart. All at once she thought of a cunning plan. She fetched her knitting needles and wool and began to knit as fast as she could.

"What on earth are you doing?" cried Fionn, "knitting at a time like this! We need a plan."

"This is the plan, Fionn, look at what I'm making."

Fionn looked and saw she was making baby clothes, truly enormous baby clothes!

"And how is this supposed to help me?" asked Fionn.

"Isn't it obvious!" said Una. "Now, go outside quickly and make a huge cradle, one big enough for yourself to fit in."

Fionn wasn't sure it was obvious at all but he would trust his wife with anything. He went into the yard and fashioned a vast cradle out of scrap wood. The finished product was a little haphazard but he had made a passable cradle.

He grabbed the cradle and ran back upstairs immediately. As he was running he heard the massive rumbling footfalls of Benandonner outside the castle. Boom! Boom! Boom!

"He's nearly here!" yelled Fionn, running into the bedroom.

"Quick!" cried Una, "put these on!"

He stared as she handed him a huge knitted dress, a bonnet and a pair of giant brogeens. Fionn did as he was told, looking completely ridiculous in the baby clothes.

There came an almighty knocking at the front door. Bang! Bang! Bang!

"Fionn Mac Cumhaill, I have come for your blood," thundered Benandonner outside. "We shall see once and for all who is the mightiest giant!"

"All right, Fionn get into the cradle and I'll open the window. Make sure you pull the dress up so he can't see your beard!" Una urged.

Fionn jumped into the cradle and covered up his beard. He looked like the world's biggest and ugliest baby!

Una threw open the windows. "Greetings, O great Benandonner!" she cried. Benandonner stomped over and stuck his head through the window. "Where is Fionn?" he roared. Spit flew all over Una but she stood her ground. "Where is my next victim?" The force of Benandonner's voice nearly knocked Una over.

"I'm afraid Fionn's hunting in the woods right now over in County Derry. It is such a pity he's not here. He was so looking forward to your fight. But he will gladly fight you when he is home. You must be tired from travelling all the way across the sea. Please do wait here but could you keep your voice down? The baby is sleeping."

Benandonner cast a giant eye around the room and saw Fionn in the cradle.

"Is that your baby?" asked Benandonner, looking alarmed.

"Yes," said Una, smiling. "He's only small now but he'll grow to be just as big as his father one day."

Benandonner had never seen such a huge baby in his life. If the baby was that large the father must be a giant beyond even himself. Fear gripped him and Benandonner ran and ran as fast as his giant legs would carry him. He didn't stop to look back but sprinted across the causeway. As he was running across it he had a sudden thought.

What if Fionn followed him across? Immediately he began ripping up the stones behind him and throwing them into the sea. By the time he got back to Scotland there were just a few stones jutting out from the Antrim coast into the sea. And this is all that's left of the Giant's Causeway.

Deirdre of the Sorrows

Once, long ago in Ulster there lived a royal storyteller named Fedlimid Mac Daill. When Fedlimid's first daughter Deirdre was born he wished to know what the story of her life would be, so he asked the wisest druid in the castle for a prophecy. When the druid laid a hand on the tiny Deirdre he withdrew it quickly, as though scalded.

"My dear fellow," he said, "your daughter will cause much trouble in her life. She will grow to be the most beautiful woman in all Ulster but she will be the death of many men."

When the Red Branch Knights of Ulster heard of this prophecy they all feared for their lives. They went to King Conor and demanded that the baby Deirdre be killed. But King Conor was a cruel and greedy man, and if the girl grew up to be as beautiful as the druid said she would he wanted her for his wife.

"Kill an innocent baby?" said the king. "Surely there must be another way?" He thought for a moment in mock puzzlement. "I know, here's what we shall do. Deirdre will be brought up far from here and when she is old enough she will marry me."

So Deirdre was taken away deep into the woods and left in the care of a wise old woman, a poet named Leabharcham.

As Deirdre grew older she became just as beautiful as the druid had foretold. Her hair was as bright and fair as sunshine and her eyes were as blue as the ocean. Leabharcham raised Deirdre well, teaching her poetry and the ways of the forest, and made sure they were never discovered. Deirdre grew up in total seclusion. In her whole life she had never met anyone other than Leabharcham. In time she grew very lonely and was desperate to meet someone, anyone. One night Deirdre had a dream about a man with hair as black as a raven, skin as white as snow and cheeks as red as roses.

When Deirdre told Leabharcham about her dream the old woman looked worried. The man in the dream sounded very familiar.

"What is it, Leabharcham, why do you frown?" said Deirdre.

"It so happens that I know that man from your dream," she replied, "His name is Naoise, one of the sons of Uisneach. He is a warrior, a hunter and a singer."

"Where can I find him?" asked Deirdre, excited.

"I cannot say, it is too dangerous for you to meet him," said Leabharcham.

But Deirdre begged Leabharcham to send for Naoise. For days she pestered her, wearing her down little by little. Leabharcham finally relented. Deirdre was like her own daughter and she could not bear to see her so sad and lonely, so she decided to send for Naoise, who came immediately when he was given the message.

As soon as Deirdre and Naoise met they fell in love. Deirdre knew she could not marry King Conor; her heart belonged to Naoise completely.

"We must go, Naoise, far, far away from Ulster. I want to marry you and no other."

That night Deirdre and Naoise left under the cover of darkness. They met up with Naoise's brothers Áinle and Ardán for protection and they travelled together for many miles seeking refuge. No one in Ireland wanted to help them. They all knew Deirdre was betrothed to King Conor and they feared his wrath. So Deirdre and the brothers left Ireland and set sail for Scotland. They settled down on a small island and for a time they led a happy life, hunting and fishing and swimming in lakes. Deirdre and Naoise married and fell deeper and deeper in love.

King Conor, humiliated and furious, eventually tracked them down. Pretending he had forgiven them, he sent a messenger, Fergus Mac Róich, asking them to come home.

Deirdre was blessed with second sight and she knew the invitation was a trap.

"Naoise, I am sure this invitation will be the death of us."

"Nonsense," said Naoise. "Fergus Mac Róich is a decent man, renowned for his honesty. He would let no harm come to us."

"Yes, and we miss Ireland and our family greatly, Deirdre. Please let us go. Much time has passed and I am sure King Conor bears us no ill will," said Ardán.

Against Deirdre's better judgement they left for Ireland with Fergus Mac Róich. Fergus Mac Róich truly was an honest and decent man and this was why King Conor had sent him. If anyone could get the girl home it was Fergus, but he also knew that Fergus would protect them all to his dying breath. With a flash of cunning Conor paid a lord to waylay Fergus. As the party arrived at the shores of Ulster the lord came down to greet them.

"Good morrow, dear friends. How are you on this fine day?"

Weary and sensing trouble, the party did nothing but grumble.

"My word, you are never Fergus Mac Róich?" said the lord. "I have heard tales of your many great deeds across the land. Please, you must come to my castle and we'll have a feast!"

King Conor knew that Fergus was honour bound to accept the lord's invitation and he would not refuse it.

"Please don't go, Fergus, please," begged Deirdre. "If you leave us now I fear something dreadful will happen."

But there was nothing Fergus could do. He had to do his duty. Deirdre and the brothers had to continue to the castle alone.

King Conor stewed as he waited. He knew if he killed Naoise and his brothers and took Deirdre for his own his reputation would be badly tarnished. He had sent them an offer of forgiveness, after all. He wanted to be quite sure that Deirdre's beauty hadn't faded first. If she had become ugly Naoise was welcome to her. King Conor called in Leabharcham as Deirdre and the brothers neared the castle.

"Go and meet our friends at the gates," he said, "I want you to tell me exactly what Deirdre looks like now."

Leabharcham did as she was ordered and met the weary travellers at the gates.

When she saw Deirdre she ran over and held her tight. It was as though not one day had passed. Deirdre was just as beautiful as ever. The years hadn't taken away from her looks.

"I have missed you greatly, Deirdre," said Leabharcham. "It is so good to see you again but I fear there is much danger for you here. Go and stay in the house of the Red Branch Knights this evening. Naoise, you and your brothers are all knights and you will be safer there by far than in the castle. Don't worry, I have a plan."

Leabharcham reported back to King Conor.

"She has become plain, my Lord, worse, ugly. The years have not been kind to her. To be honest, she's hardly worth the trouble."

King Conor did not believe her and he sent another spy, a vile man called Glenbann, to confirm what Leabharcham said.

Glenbann was not a stealthy man. He tried to spy on the party at the house of the Red Branch Knights but got caught. As he peeked through an open door he saw Deirdre playing chess with Naoise. Naoise saw him and threw a chess piece at him that took out his eye. Naoise chased after Glenbann but he escaped.

"She is just as beautiful as ever, my Lord," said Glenbann. "It was worth losing an eye just to see her."

King Conor sent his men to attack the Red Branch House immediately.

With the help of a few Red Branch Knights the sons of Uisneach fought off the king's men. Wave after wave of soldiers came but the brothers killed every soldier who attacked them. King Conor saw that his men were making no headway, the brothers were just too powerful. In desperation he went to the druid Cathbad to ask for help. Cathbad knew King Conor was not a good man so he thought long and hard before answering him.

"I will help you, my king, on one condition," said Cathbad, "that you promise you will not kill the sons of Uisneach."

"Of course, dear Cathbad. I only want Naoise to apologise and all will be forgiven," said the king with a twisted smile. Cathbad had said he could not kill the sons of Uisneach, but that didn't mean somebody else couldn't do it.

Cathbad then cast a spell that surrounded the sons of Uisneach with the force of an angry ocean. The men struggled as though they were swimming through vast waves. They fought valiantly until exhaustion overtook them and their weapons slipped from their fingers. The brothers surrounded Deirdre, protecting her, but one by one they were captured. Conor came storming into the house.

"The spy spoke true, you are just as beautiful as ever," he said to Deirdre, who was weeping upon the floor. He looked around at the Red Branch Knights. "I know these men are knights, but you all swore loyalty to me. Who will kill these men for me?" The knights hung their heads. None of them wanted to kill their brothers.

King Conor spoke again. "I will give his weight in gold to the man who kills these traitors!"

Finally a man stepped forward.

His name was Maigne Rough Hand, the son of the king of Norway, and long ago Naoise had killed his father and brothers in a battle.

"I will gladly kill these men for you, King Conor."

Deirdre begged for forgiveness but the king's heart was made of ice.

Áinle spoke up. "Kill me first, please, I am the youngest and I have never been without my brothers."

"No, kill me first," said Ardán. "I cannot bear to watch my brothers die." Then Naoise said, "Please, sir, kill us all at the same time with one stroke of your sword."

And so Maigne Rough Hand cut off the brothers' heads at the same instant.

Deirdre, broken-hearted, made no protest as King Conor led her away to his chariot. As they rode away he told her they would be married immediately.

But Deirdre could not bear the thought. Naoise was her only love and she swore she would never marry the evil king. She threw herself from the chariot and died immediately.

King Conor was never to get his heart's desire and for ever more people knew what he was.

He buried Deirdre in Emain Macha, next to where Naoise and his brothers lay. In his malice he had wooden stakes driven into the ground between their two graves. He could not bear the thought of the lovers touching each other, even in death. But the wooden stakes put down roots in the graves and grew into two beautiful trees that twined together, inseparable and one.

Diarmuid and Gráinne

Long ago when the Fianna still roamed Ireland there lived a man called Diarmuid Ó Duibhne. He was a legendary warrior and the right-hand man to Fionn Mac Cumhaill. Diarmuid was strong and loyal and a great fighter, but this was not what he was famous for. All through the land, people said that he was beautiful. And while this was obvious to any who saw him, the thing that made him truly irresistible was his Bol Sherca. This was a small magical spot on his forehead. They say all who saw it fell madly in love with Diarmuid in an instant. Diarmuid learned of this power at an early age and took to wearing his hair down to cover the spot. As wonderful as love is, it can be a dangerous thing.

Fionn Mac Cumhaill was still the greatest warrior in Ireland and the leader of the Fianna. He was getting on in years but he still led a full life of feasting, story telling and adventures with the Fianna. Only one thing was missing. Years earlier Fionn's wife had died and he had grown lonely. Fionn decided enough time had passed, that he had mourned his wife for many years and she would not have wanted him to be alone. So one day he called his most trusted men to ask for their advice.

"Men, I wish to take a new wife. Who in the Emerald Isle should I choose?" Fionn said.

The men did not have to think for long. They all agreed that the only woman worthy of their great leader was the lady Gráinne, the most beautiful woman in Ireland and the daughter of High King Cormac Mac Airt.

Now, Fionn was aware that he was a good deal older than Gráinne – he was old enough to be her father – and he was shy of asking for her hand himself, so he sent two ambassadors to speak to Gráinne on his behalf.

Gráinne had had countless proposals in the past, had been sent perfume and flowers, fabulous jewels and beautiful garments, but only one person had ever turned her head. When she was 12, Gráinne had seen a boy playing hurling outside her father's castle.

The day was turbulent and windy, full of rain then, suddenly, sun. As Gráinne watched the boy run, his hair was blown back by the wind and she had fallen instantly in love with him, utterly and completely. Years passed, and Gráinne refused every man who asked for her hand. Her love for the boy had never faltered, one glance at him had gripped her heart for ever.

She would always love the boy and she was ready to send the ambassadors away when they came. But when Gráinne heard who the proposal was from she was flattered. Fionn Mac Cumhaill was the greatest man in Ireland and the wonders of his deeds were sung across the land. She had spent long enough waiting for the boy. In any case she did not even know where he was, or if she would ever see him again. With a twinge of sadness she accepted the ambassadors' offer.

The king was delighted. His daughter had finally chosen a suitor and there could be no better man than Fionn Mac Cumhaill. He invited all the Fianna to a great feast.

Gráinne had heard the tales but she had never actually seen Fionn. Before she sat down to the feast she hid behind a curtain to try and catch a glimpse of him. There among his Fianna she saw him, tall and powerful, but certainly more than twice her age. Gráinne was a little disappointed. Then she noticed the man sitting next to him. She gasped. The man was Diarmuid Ó Duibhne. Gráinne immediately recognised him as the love of her life.

She knew instantly that she couldn't marry Fionn Mac Cumhaill. A plan formed in her mind. She entered the feast slowly with a goblet of wine into which she'd put a sleeping posset. All eyes turned to her as she approached the high table shyly.

"My husband to be," she said to Fionn, "it is a joy to meet you. This is the finest wine in the kingdom. Please, I offer you a drink from my cup."

Fionn smiled widely, for the lady was just as beautiful as he had heard. "Certainly I will drink, my lady," he said, and he drank deeply. As soon as he put down the cup his eyelids drooped and he fell asleep.

Gráinne turned to Diarmuid and proclaimed her love for him.

"Please, sir, leave with me tonight, there is nothing more that my heart desires than to be with you."

Diarmuid was flabbergasted. Gráinne was the most beautiful woman he had ever seen but he could not betray Fionn. He thought hard for a moment.

"My lady, I cannot," he said finally. "I cannot betray my friend."

Gráinne turned to Diarmuid and put him under a geasa, a spell, which would oblige him to run away with her.

"But Fionn is my leader, he is like a father to me."

"You would refuse a geasa from me?" asked Gráinne.

"The lady speaks true, Diarmuid," said Fionn's son Oisín. "You cannot refuse a geasa from a lady, especially not the high king's daughter."

Diarmuid knew he was right even if it would tear his heart in two. And so, a broken man, he ran away with Gráinne.

In her dreams Gráinne thought running away with Diarmuid would be terribly romantic, but she was unused to travelling and grew weary within a few miles. Gráinne asked Diarmuid to carry her. He refused, hoping she might go back to Fionn.

At that moment Aengus Óg, the god of love, appeared on the road before them.

"Two weary travellers I see, but you travel with love. Let me help you on your way." And Aengus Óg conjured up two horses for them to escape on.

"Be warned, Fionn will soon wake and he will come after you. Some advice I give you. Never sleep in a cave with one opening, never a house with one door, never a tree with one branch. Never eat where you cook and never sleep where you eat. The road is your friend. Stay ever on it to be one step ahead of Fionn."

Back at the castle Fionn was stirring. When his men told him what Diarmuid had done he flew into a rage.

"That traitorous little imp, I'll have him for this! Men, make ready the horses!"

Fionn's men tried to explain about the geasa but Fionn didn't care. Diarmuid had betrayed him and he would pay. Fionn chased after the pair with his Fianna. They searched for days, until the days became weeks, and then until the weeks became months.

Diarmuid and Gráinne had heeded Aengus Óg's advice, moving constantly from place to place. For a whole year they evaded Fionn and the Fianna, but the Fianna were closing in. Everywhere they found small traces the couple had left behind, fires and fish bones and small nests they had made to sleep in. These clues led them closer and closer, until one night they located the couple in a house with seven doors. Assured that they had found the perfect hiding place Diarmuid and Gráinne slept easily that night. However, members of the Fianna were blocking each door so they couldn't escape.

Aengus Óg appeared to them inside the house, "Wake!" he said.

Diarmuid sat bolt upright.

"You are both in grave danger. You must leave now. Come let me spirit you away."

Diarmuid roused Gráinne. "Quick, you must go with Aengus Óg, the Fianna are at the door."

"Will you not come with me, my love?" Gráinne asked.

"Alas. I cannot, I must face Fionn and beg forgiveness for what I have done."

Gráinne pleaded with Diarmuid to come but his mind was made up, "Go now!" And with that Aengus Óg whisked Gráinne magically away.

Diarmuid then opened each door in turn. At every door he came across a stony-faced Fianna member who refused to let him pass. The seventh door was guarded by Fionn himself. When Diarmuid opened it Fionn roared in anger and advanced on him. All the Fianna members entered the house and they surrounded Diarmuid.

But Diarmuid was fast and nimble and as they closed in he leaped clean over their heads and escaped to join Gráinne.

Fionn was furious. He had missed his chance for revenge. He carried on looking for years, but he never managed to find Gráinne and Diarmuid again.

They stayed constantly on the run. They even raised five children, moving from place to place and never knowing a home. Exhausted and outcast, Gráinne and Diarmuid knew this feud must come to an end. Enough time had passed and Fionn's anger had abated a little, so the couple decided to try and make amends. They went to Fionn's castle with all their children and threw themselves on his mercy.

Fionn decided to put his anger aside. When he saw the family, bedraggled, tired and dirty, his heart was overcome with pity. He agreed to put the matter to rest and welcomed them back with a great feast. The family were finally able to be at peace, and in time Diarmuid and Fionn rebuilt their friendship.

Many years passed and one day Fionn and Diarmuid decided to go hunting. While out in the woods they came across a gigantic boar.

"I've never seen anything like it before," said Diarmuid.

"Nor I," said Fionn. "It is fully twice the size of any boar I have seen before. We must have it for a feast!"

The men cornered the boar and the beast ran straight at Diarmuid.

"Diarmuid, be careful!" yelled Fionn. Diarmuid took a giant swing with his sword but it wasn't enough. He had managed to kill the beast but not before it had gored him in the stomach. Diarmuid sank, dying, to the forest floor.

"Fionn, please, my friend, allow me to drink from your hands," Diarmuid gasped, for he knew that anyone who drank water from the hands of Fionn Mac Cumhaill would be healed because of his magical thumb.

Fionn ran to the river and carried back water to Diarmuid. His old friend lay panting on the ground a second away from death. He leant down to save him but at the last moment Fionn stopped. All the bitterness he had felt towards Diarmuid came rushing back and he let the water trickle between his fingers. As soon as he had done it the bitterness left him. Fionn rushed back to the pool to collect more water but by the time he returned it was too late. Diarmuid Ó Duibhne was dead upon the ground.

Oisín and Niamh in Tír na nÓg

Long ago, when Ireland was young and the world was fresh and new, there lived a noble warrior called Oisín. Oisín's father was the legendary Fionn Mac Cumhaill himself. Like his father, Oisín was the leader of the Fianna, the protectors of Ireland and the king.

One fine day the Fianna were hunting deer around Lough Leane. They stopped by the waterside to rest and in the distance they saw a woman approaching on a snow-white horse. The men thought the horse was most strange for her hooves made no sound against the ground.

As the woman came closer the Fianna saw that she was the most beautiful woman any of them had ever seen. Her long golden hair shimmered to her waist, her skin was as smooth as alabaster and her eyes sparkled like bright blue sapphires. A light emanated from her as she rode, some secret power that set her all aglow. She rode up to the Fianna and stopped before them.

Oisín stepped forward, half in a trance. "Fair maiden, where have you come from? Please won't you tell us your name?" he asked.

When the woman spoke her voice was musical and quiet but they heard every word. "I am Niamh of the Golden Hair, daughter of the king of Tír na nÓg. I have heard tell of a great warrior named Oisín who lives here. I have heard of his great deeds, that he is brave and worthy and a man of song and poetry."

Oisín was stunned. "My lady, I am the man you seek. I am Oisín, son of Fionn Mac Cumhaill."

Niamh cast a radiant smile down at him. "Then I have come to find you and ask you a question. I come from the land of eternal youth. It is a joyous place where there is no fear and no sorrow. Any wish your heart desires will be yours immediately. There is no death and our people never age. Will you go with me, Oisín? Will you join me in Tír na nÓg?"

Oisín looked back at his men, with whom he'd shared so much. How would they fare without him? He looked around at his country that he loved so dearly. Could he leave his birthplace? He would be heartbroken to leave, but one glance at Niamh told him where his heart truly belonged. He had loved her from the first second he saw her.

"I gladly accept your offer, Niamh of Tír na nÓg. I will go with you to the land of eternal youth."

Niamh offered her hand to Oisín and he jumped onto the back of the snow-white horse.

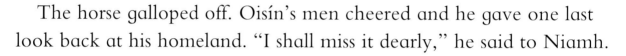

The horse's coat felt like the world's finest silk, and when Oisín sat back it felt as though he were floating. He waved his hand to the Fianna.

"Dear friends, my destiny has called, but fear not, I shall return soon. We will meet again."

The horse galloped off. Oisín's men cheered and he gave one last look back at his homeland. "I shall miss it dearly," he said to Niamh.

"Just wait until you see Tír na nÓg. It is a world of poetry, music and light. There are pools of salmon and orchards creaking with golden apples. The trees are ever in bloom and bees dance over the multicoloured plains. The air is heavy with a sweetness no mortal can know."

As they rode Oisín noticed that the horse's hooves never quite touched the ground. They skimmed over rock and grass and as they approached the ocean the horse did not stop but ran clear over the waves.

A path of pure sunlight guided their way. A lifetime later, or it could have been no time at all, they arrived at the magical shores of Tír na nÓg. The king and queen received Oisín with happy hearts. They had never seen their daughter smiling as she did now.

"A wise choice, my daughter. What a strong and handsome man you have found," said the queen.

"You will enjoy your life here Oisín," said the king. "Anything your heart desires, you can do. Welcome to Tír na nÓg."

There were streams and brooks, great lakes and mountains. The fields of flowers ran on for ever. Animals gambolled in the fields and everywhere smiling faces appeared to greet Oisín. Every face was as beautiful as the last. Golden light shone over everything and everyone. The sight was almost too beautiful to comprehend. As soon as Oisín's feet touched the ground he felt every worry in the world leave him. Niamh dismounted and took his hand.

"I am so glad to bring you to my home. It is your home now too," she said, smiling broadly at him.

Oisín felt he was the happiest man in the world. That night the king and queen held a great feast in his honour.

The feast was a marvel. There was music and dancing and twinkling lights shone from a canopy that looked like stars. There were a thousand different dishes from every corner of the land, a fountain of wine and a cake the size of an elephant. There were many speeches and many toasts. The festival went on for days, and when it ended Oisín felt he was truly home.

Oisín and Niamh fell madly in love and they were married within a few days. Their life together was filled with joy and no two souls anywhere where a better match.

For a long, long while time passed very happily for Oisín. He spent his days hunting and writing poetry. In the evenings he feasted and sang with Niamh until sleep took them. His life was full of light and song and all the joy a person can know.

One of Oisín's favourite pastimes was to tell stories of his father Fionn, the Fianna and Ireland. Every evening he would regale people with these fabulous tales and the crowds listened eagerly. While he enjoyed telling the stories he also found there was a tinge of sadness. As time went on he began to miss his family and Ireland more and more. But time does not pass in Tír na nÓg as it does in the mortal world. An hour can feel like a second. Before Oisín knew it 300 years had passed. Soon his longing to return to his homeland overcame his love for Tír na nÓg. One evening he told Niamh that he had to return to the mortal world.

"My love, I do not want you to go. I shall miss you greatly," she said.

"And I miss my homeland greatly. I shall return and it will only feel like a moment in this world, my darling."

A tear fell from Niamh's eye. "If you must go, you must go. Take my horse, but I warn you, never dismount. If your foot touches mortal soil you will never be able to return to Tír na nÓg again."

"I promise," said Oisín, "I shall not take one step on the emerald ground."

Oisín kissed his wife and set off for Ireland straight away. Every second he remained time was racing ahead in the mortal world. Oisín mounted Niamh's horse and galloped off to his homeland. He urged the horse on to greater and greater speeds until they were flying across the ocean and over the land until Oisín could see the green fields of his youth.

Ireland stretched out before him, almost as wondrous as Tír na nÓg. Oisín rode for his father's castle as fast as he could. When he saw his home in the distance his heart leaped, but as he drew closer it fell to the pit of his stomach. The castle was crumbling and falling into ruin. Oisín rode to the doors and knocked but there was no answer. The castle was as quiet as the grave.

Oisín took off in a panic. A terrible thought had seized him and he rode on and on, desperately searching for a sight of his father or the Fianna. But the further he rode the further his heart sank. Everywhere he saw change. The faces were different, the buildings were new. This was not the Ireland that he had known. As he passed through Gleann na Smól, the Valley of the Thrushes, despair overtook him and he slowed to a listless walk.

"You there, sir, we're in need of a strong man," a voice called.

Oisín looked up and saw a group of men trying to move a boulder.

"We must move this boulder so our cart can pass through the valley," another man said.

Oisín trotted over to help. He could not step down so he leant from his saddle to move the stone, but as he did so the saddle strap broke. Oisín yelled as he fell to the ground.

Immediately the snow-white horse galloped away, leaving Oisín lying in the grass. The men drew back in horror. Before their eyes Oisín became withered and ancient, ageing 300 years in an instant.

Oisín explained to the men about Tír na nÓg and the magical horse and how he would never be able to return to his love. The men were deeply saddened by the story and immediately took Oisín to see St Patrick, the wisest man they knew. But wise as St Patrick was he was powerless to help.

"I cannot send you back to Tír na nÓg, Oisín. The men who brought you here mean well, but they do not understand that I am just a man."

Oisín bowed his ancient head gravely, then asked the question he feared most.

"Sir, please tell me what has become of the Fianna, what has become of my father Fionn Mac Cumhaill?"

St Patrick laid a comforting hand on Oisín's shoulder.

"My son, I am so sorry, but they have long since left this world."

It was as Oisín feared and his heart was filled with a terrible sadness. "Your father lives on in heaven," said St Patrick, "and he and the Fianna live on in you, in memory. Tell me about your father, and all your days with the Fianna."

And so Oisín spoke late into the night of his days alongside the Fianna. He spoke of his father, Fionn Mac Cumhaill, not just of his many great deeds but of their times together as father and son, when they hunted and feasted, when they heard tales and songs. He spoke of his life in Tír na nÓg and his beautiful wife. Oisín talked and talked until his ancient body was utterly spent and then he lay back and died. He never returned to Tír na nÓg, but the story of Oisín and Niamh will live on for ever.

Setanta becomes Cúchulainn

Long ago, in ancient Ireland, there lived a boy named Setanta. He was a demigod, the son of the mighty god Lugh himself. Some even say he was the very incarnation of Lugh. But greatness ran on both sides of Setanta's family.

His uncle, Conor Mac Nessa, was the mighty king of Ulster. The king lived in a great fort near the town of Armagh at a place called Emain Macha.

Conor Mac Nessa had a troop of boys, the Macra, under his care. He gave the boys a playing field and all the weapons they could desire. The boys were taught to wrestle and run, to train with sword and spear, to play at war as ferociously as they played at their hurling. This was the training ground for the Red Branch Knights, Conor's legendary army. Setanta longed to join the knights, just as he longed to join the Macra.

Setanta lived a quiet life with his mother in Dundalk. Quiet, except for a repeated question.

"Mother, please let me join the Macra," Setanta begged for the thousandth time. "I'm the fastest boy in Dundalk and the strongest. And you said yourself I am the bravest."

"You're too young, my son," said Setanta's mother with a sigh of exhaustion.

"But mother, I must join the Macra, otherwise I shall never be a great warrior."

"A great warrior must first learn patience, my son. Learn that and you will go."

Setanta refrained from asking his mother again for a whole year. One day, when his birthday was near, Setanta's mother asked what he would like as a gift.

Setanta took a deep breath and said, "Mother, I have grown over the past year and I have learned patience. I would like to join the Macra."

Setanta's mother smiled sadly. Her son was still young and she would miss him dearly, but there was a fierce determination burning in his eyes that she could not bear to put out.

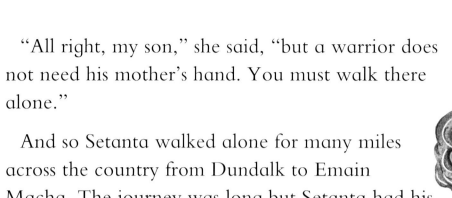

"All right, my son," she said, "but a warrior does not need his mother's hand. You must walk there alone."

And so Setanta walked alone for many miles across the country from Dundalk to Emain Macha. The journey was long but Setanta had his hurley and sliotar to pass the time. He would cast the sliotar far ahead and race to catch it with his hurley before it hit the ground. Again and again he did this, constantly chasing after his sliotar and never missing. Setanta reached Emain Macha in a matter of days, tired but exhilarated. Across the fields he saw the rippling flags of his uncle's fort caught high in the breeze. His heart sang. This was where he was meant to be.

As Setanta neared the fort he saw the boys of the Macra playing a game of hurling below the walls. They played furiously and faster than Setanta had ever seen. All the boys at his old school seemed sluggish and lazy by comparison. But Setanta was no average schoolboy, he was the son of a god. He ran over and caught the ball. This angered the Macra boys. They were furious that Setanta had joined in their game without invitation. They attacked him from all sides, throwing spears at him. Faster than an arrow Setanta grabbed a shield and caught the spears upon it. In a rage the boys charged at him, but the young boy was quicker, braver and more agile than any of them. He fought them off one by one.

The king, who was engaged in a game of chess upstairs, was most angry about the noise. He thrust his head out of the window.

"What on earth is all the racket about?" he demanded. The boys all stopped fighting immediately, and looked to the ground in shame. "Well?" said the king.

Setanta shouted up to his uncle, "I am your nephew. I have come from Dundalk to join the Macra."

The king appraised his nephew far beneath him. He squinted. All the boys below appeared dirty and bruised, all apart from Setanta.

"Did you fight the whole of my Macra yourself?"

"Yes, my king," Setanta said.

"Then you are worthy indeed. It would be my honour to have you, nephew."

So, to Setanta's delight, he joined the famed Macra. He learned their ways and played their games and became the greatest student the Macra had ever known.

Setanta loved his life in the Macra and time passed quickly as contented time does.

Not so far from Emain Macha lived a wealthy blacksmith called Culann who made swords and spears for the king and his warriors. One day Culann invited the king and his knights to a grand feast at his house to thank the king for his years of orders.

The king and his knights made ready to leave for the house that evening. Just as they were about to depart the king called for Setanta. Setanta was the bravest boy he had ever met and his greatest pupil. He was very keen to show him off. He found him playing a game of hurling with the other Macra boys.

"Setanta! Come here," the king yelled.

Setanta stopped playing immediately and ran over to his uncle.

"What service do you require of me, my king?" asked Setanta, bowing.

"Rise and come with me to a feast. You are my bravest and fiercest pupil and I wish to have you at my side tonight."

"As you wish, my king, but it would be bad form to leave the game a player short. May I finish and join you later? I can run very fast."

The king agreed and set off with his knights for Culann's house in merry spirits.

Culann was delighted to see the king and his knights.

"My king! How glad I am to see you! Without you I could never have afforded this fine house. Tonight it is yours! Please enter with your knights and make merry!"

The king and his knights all cheered and there was much drinking and toasting as they entered the house.

Before the feast was due to begin, Culann called above the roaring crowd. "My dear men, I must ask if everyone is inside the house, for I must release my hound to guard the house as we eat."

This hound was no ordinary hound. He was a beast. It took three chains, each held by three men, just to hold him. The people of Ulster feared him greatly and none ever dreamed of robbing Culann.

"Yes!" cried the king, "we're all in, release the beast!" But in his drunken state the king had completely forgotten about his nephew. Setanta had left Emain Macha as soon as his game had finished but this had left him a clear mile behind the king's party. Setanta hastened to join the king and ran with all his might. As soon as he arrived outside Culann's house he heard the dreadful growls of a wolfhound. Suddenly the monstrous hound leapt out of the bushes and advanced on Setanta, his hackles up.

Setanta looked around for a weapon to defend himself with but all he had were his hurley and sliotar. The hound was upon him. Jaws wide, the beast flew at the young boy. Without a second thought Setanta hurled his sliotar down the hound's throat with all his might.

His aim was true. The ball lodged in the hound's throat so that he choked and could not breathe. All was very quiet and Setanta let out a sigh of relief. The hound lay dead upon the ground.

The feast inside was in full flow when suddenly the king jumped up. "We've forgotten Setanta!" he yelled in despair. The king and his knights rushed out of Culann's house. The king looked this way and that, expecting to see the boy torn to pieces. When he saw Setanta standing over the fallen hound the king gasped in astonishment.

"Quite a boy, indeed, my nephew. One day you shall make a fine Red Branch Knight."

"No!" cried Culann who had just seen his hound dead upon the ground. "My hound!" Culann ran over and knelt by his dog, stroking his head. "I am very sorry that you had to fight my hound, Setanta, and I'm very glad you are all right. It's just that he was my favourite pet and my companion."

Setanta looked at the sadness in Culann's eyes and his heart broke.

"I am most sorry, Culann. I don't know how I can ever make this up to you." Setanta had an idea. "How about this, as I have robbed you of your guard dog I will be your guard dog until you have reared a new pup."

Culann gladly accepted, for any boy who could defeat his hound was a worthy guard indeed.

The king was sad to lose Setanta but he knew it was for the best. The king laughed. "My greatest student, a guard dog! And a great guard you shall make. All hail Cúchulainn!" The king cried.

"Hail Cúchulainn" The Red Branch Knights roared.

Setanta looked confused. "Uncle, what does Cúchulainn mean?"

The king put his hand on Setanta's shoulder, "It means Hound of Culann!" Setanta smiled, because he quite liked his new nickname.

The king and his knights departed, leaving Setanta to his guard duty.

Setanta performed his duties with grace and bravery and became the best guard Culann had ever had, far better than any dog. He went on to perform many great deeds and became the greatest ever warrior of the Red Branch Knights. And ever afterwards Setanta was known as Cúchulainn.